W9-BTF-665

Remy Charlip

BABY HEARTS AND BABY FLOWERS

GREENWILLOW BOOKS
AN IMPRINT OF HARPERCOLLINS PUBLISHERS

DEDICATED TO LISA MARIE WEIMER

BABY HEARTS AND BABY FLOWERS
COPYRIGHT © 2002 BY REMY CHARLIP
ALL RIGHTS RESERVED.
PRINTED IN SINGAPORE BY TIEN WAH PRESS.
WWW.HARPERCHILDRENS.COM

WATERCOLOR WASHES ON ARCHES PAPER WERE
USED FOR THE FULL-COLOR ART.
THE TEXT TYPE IS ALBERTUS.

LIBRARY OF CONGRESS CATALOGING-IN-PUBLICATION DATA
CHARLIP, REMY.
BABY HEARTS AND BABY FLOWERS / BY REMY CHARLIP.
    P.   CM.
"GREENWILLOW BOOKS."
SUMMARY: A RHYMED TALE DESCRIBING ALL SORTS OF BABIES
AND THINGS ASSOCIATED WITH BABIES, ENDING WITH A BABY
BED AND A WISH FOR SWEET DREAMS.
ISBN 0-06-029591-0 (TRADE). ISBN 0-06-029592-9 (LIB. BDG.)
[I. BABIES—FICTION. 2. BEDTIME—FICTION. 3. STORIES IN RHYME.]
I. TITLE.   PZ8.3.C386 BAB 2002   [E]—DC21   2001023671

10 9 8 7 6 5 4 3 2 1
FIRST EDITION

AND BABY FLOWERS.

BABY CLOUDS

AND BABY SHOWERS.

BABY BUNNIES,

PUPPIES, KITTENS,

ALL IN FUNNY HATS

AND MITTENS.

BABY BOOKS AND BABY TOYS

FOR

BABY GIRLS AND BABY BOYS.

BABY TABLE, BABY CHAIR.

BABIES...

BABIES...EVERYWHERE.

BABY PILLOW, BABY BED.

NICE SOFT PLACE

TO REST YOUR HEAD.

GO TO SLEEP NOW,

TREES

MOON AND STARS,

AND HOUSES, BEES AND CARS.

GO TO SLEEP, MY LITTLE ONE.

SLEEP

AND DREAM NOW, DAY IS DONE.

Remy Charlip

SAYS HE WAS FORTUNATE TO HAVE BEGUN HIS CAREER
ILLUSTRATING THE WORK OF TWO BRILLIANT PICTURE BOOK
PIONEERS: MARGARET WISE BROWN (THE DEAD BIRD)
AND RUTH KRAUSS (A MOON OR A BUTTON).
IN 1957 HIS OWN PICTURE BOOK WHERE IS EVERYBODY?
WAS CHOSEN BY THE NEW YORK PUBLIC LIBRARY
AS A "DISTINGUISHED READER," ALONG WITH THE CAT IN THE HAT
AND LITTLE BEAR. SINCE THEN HE HAS DONE MORE THAN
THIRTY BOOKS, INCLUDING SUCH MODERN CLASSICS
AS FORTUNATELY, I LOVE YOU, ARM IN ARM,
AND, MORE RECENTLY, SLEEPYTIME RHYME.
HIS AWARDS INCLUDE A BOSTON GLOBE-HORN BOOK AWARD,
BEST PICTURE BOOK AT THE BOLOGNA BOOK FAIR,
AND THREE INCLUSIONS IN THE NEW YORK TIMES
"TEN BEST ILLUSTRATED BOOKS OF THE YEAR."

HE WAS HONORED BY THE LIBRARY OF CONGRESS
IN AN EVENING "CELEBRATION OF REMY CHARLIP,"
AND WITH A MAJOR EXHIBITION OF HIS PAINTINGS
AND DRAWINGS AT THE SAN FRANCISCO MAIN LIBRARY,
WHERE HE WAS ALSO NAMED A "LITERARY LAUREATE"
AND THEIR FIRST "ARTIST IN RESIDENCE."

REMY CHARLIP LIVES IN SAN FRANCISCO, CALIFORNIA.
WWW.REMYCHARLIP.COM

Norfolk Public Library

0 1186 0806967 0

NO LONGER PROPERTY OF
NORFOLK PUBLIC LIBRARY

10/09

PRETLOW BRANCH
Norfolk Public Library

DEMCO